03/2013

DISCARD

Dear Parents and Educators,

Welcome to Penguin Young Readers! As parents and educators, you know that each child develops at his or her own pace—in terms of speech, critical thinking, and, of course, reading. Penguin Young Readers recognizes this fact. As a result, each Penguin Young Readers book is assigned a traditional easy-to-read level (1–4) as well as a Guided Reading Level (A–P). Both of these systems will help you choose the right book for your child. Please refer to the back of each book for specific leveling information. Penguin Young Readers features esteemed authors and illustrators, stories about favorite characters, fascinating nonfiction, and more!

Lucky Goes to School!

LEVEL 2

GUIDED READING LEVEL **E**

This book is perfect for a **Progressing Reader** who:
- can figure out unknown words by using picture and context clues;
- can recognize beginning, middle, and ending sounds;
- can make and confirm predictions about what will happen in the text; and
- can distinguish between fiction and nonfiction.

Here are some **activities** you can do during and after reading this book:
- Sight Words: Sight words are frequently used words that readers must know just by looking at them. Knowing these words helps children develop into efficient readers. As you read the story, point out the sight words below.

can	go	is	the	up
first	his	new	to	walk

- Make Predictions: Lucky does not think he can have fun without his owner during the school day, but he has a great time with some new dog friends at the park. Still, at the end of the day, Lucky is happy to be back with his owner. What do you think Lucky will do when his owner goes to school the next day? Do you think he will have fun?

Remember, sharing the love of reading with a child is the best gift you can give!

—Bonnie Bader, EdM
   Penguin Young Readers program

*Penguin Young Readers are leveled by independent reviewers applying the standards developed by Irene Fountas and Gay Su Pinnell in *Matching Books to Readers: Using Leveled Books in Guided Reading*, Heinemann, 1999.

For Sam, who is starting kindergarten—GH

To Joy—NG

Penguin Young Readers
Published by the Penguin Group
Penguin Group (USA) Inc., 375 Hudson Street, New York, New York 10014, USA
Penguin Group (Canada), 90 Eglinton Avenue East, Suite 700, Toronto, Ontario M4P 2Y3, Canada
(a division of Pearson Penguin Canada Inc.)
Penguin Books Ltd., 80 Strand, London WC2R 0RL, England
Penguin Group Ireland, 25 St. Stephen's Green, Dublin 2, Ireland (a division of Penguin Books Ltd.)
Penguin Group (Australia), 250 Camberwell Road, Camberwell, Victoria 3124, Australia
(a division of Pearson Australia Group Pty. Ltd.)
Penguin Books India Pvt. Ltd., 11 Community Centre, Panchsheel Park, New Delhi—110 017, India
Penguin Group (NZ), 67 Apollo Drive, Rosedale, Auckland 0632, New Zealand
(a division of Pearson New Zealand Ltd.)
Penguin Books (South Africa) (Pty.) Ltd., 24 Sturdee Avenue,
Rosebank, Johannesburg 2196, South Africa

Penguin Books Ltd., Registered Offices: 80 Strand, London WC2R 0RL, England

Text copyright © 2001 by Gail Herman. Illustrations copyright © 2001 by Norman Gorbaty. All rights
reserved. First published in 2001 by Grosset & Dunlap, an imprint of Penguin Group (USA) Inc.
Published in 2012 by Penguin Young Readers, an imprint of Penguin Group (USA) Inc.,
345 Hudson Street, New York, New York 10014. Manufactured in China.

Library of Congress Control Number: 2001270031

ISBN 978-0-448-42498-9   10 9 8 7 6 5 4 3 2 1

PENGUIN YOUNG READERS

LEVEL
PROGRESSING
READER
2

Lucky Goes to School!

by Gail Herman
illustrated by Norman Gorbaty

Penguin Young Readers
An Imprint of Penguin Group (USA) Inc.

Lucky wakes up.

Something is new today.

Something is different.

"Hurry up, Lucky,"
his boy tells him.
"Today is the first day
of school."

Lucky is sad.

What will Lucky do all day?

"Come, Lucky,"
says his boy.
"You can walk
to school with me."

Lucky and his boy

go down the street.

Now they are at school.

"Good boy,"

says his boy.

He hugs Lucky.

"I will see you soon."

15

Lucky does not think he can

have fun without his boy.

Lucky sees lots of boys and girls.

Lucky sees lots of dogs.

"Good-bye," say the kids.

The dogs wag their tails,

but they look sad, too.

Lucky goes to the park.

There are the other dogs.

Lucky wags his tail.

He wants the other dogs

to play with him.

All the dogs wag their tails.

Yes! They do want to play.

23

The dogs play

"pass the stick."

They chase each other.

They have a snack.

They splash in the mud

and make paw print pictures.

Then they have a nap.

Lucky thinks about his boy.

Lucky hopes his boy

is having fun at school.

Now it is time to go.

Lucky wags his tail again.

He is saying good-bye to

his new friends.

30

Lucky goes back to school.

He is with his boy again.

Lucky and his boy walk home.

They are happy.

Tomorrow is another

day of school.